Syrynn
Don't Fear the Dark

Syrynn
Don't Fear the Dark

Written & Illustrated by
Kristin Ann Calderon

HAWAII WAY PUBLISHING

HAWAII WAY PUBLISHING
4118 West Harold Ct., Visalia, CA 93291
www.HAWAIIWAYPUBLISHING.com

HAWAII Way logo and name/acronym, (Health And Wealth And Inspired Ideas), are registered and trademarked by HAWAII Way Publishing.

The right of *Kristin Ann Calderon* to be identified as the Author of the work has been asserted by her in accordance with the Copyright, Designs and
Patents Act 1988. **All rights reserved.**

No part of this publication may be reproduced, distributed, or transmitted in any form or by any means, including photocopying, recording, or other electronic or mechanical methods without the prior and express written permission of the author of each chapter, or the publisher, except in the case of brief quotations embodied in critical reviews and certain other noncommercial uses permitted by copyright law. HAWAII Way Author/Speakers Division can send authors to your live event.

For more information or to book an event contact HAWAII Way Publishing at HAWAIIWaypublishing@gmail.com, or 559-972-4168
Printed in the United States of America
ISBN 978-1-945384-30-1

Copyright© 2017 Kristin Ann Calderon, South Lake Tahoe, CA

DEDICATION

To my childhood and all my friends and family,

and to Spyro, for giving me my love of dragons.

ACKNOWLEDGEMENTS

A special thanks to Jonah, Chase, Zach, Shawn, Brooklyn, and my parents for letting me create dragons for them and for this story when I was young. My first and second grade teacher, Mrs. Majarian, for encouraging my silly stories and believing in my skills as a future writer, and to Season Burch for helping me make my dreams a reality. Also, a special thank you to Julie B. Burdine for the front cover illustration. You have an amazing talent for art.

PROLOGUE

It was a calm night, raining softly as the mist shrouded the cracked wasteland like a veil and the moon cast rays of light over the craggy canyons. All was quiet.

Except for the purple terror of a dragon falling out of the sky like a shooting star, spiraling to the ground, and destroying everything in his wake. He groaned as he pushed himself to his feet, the six white, curved horns on his head scraping a canyon wall and raining dirt down on his body.

His deep red eyes glanced around, looking for any sign of his pursuers. So far, so good. His torn leather wings folded in tight against his back as he started to limp forward. His tail, decorated with an abundance of sharp spines, swayed from side to side and brushed away any footprints he left in the mud, the rain smoothing out the rest. At this pace, it was going to be a long night.

His petal-shaped ears behind his horns perked up as he heard a screech in the distance. "Fantastic. Thought I'd lost them in the fog." The dragon crawled into an uncomfortably tight crevice in the floor, twisting his lithe body until he finally vanished from sight, his tail slipping inside just as three flying snake-like creatures soared overhead, spitting fireballs to light their way in the dense fog. Once they were out of sight, he finally let out a sigh of relief.

He wriggled violently, trying to free himself, but he

was squeezed in tight. Sometimes it sucked to be a large flying reptile. He squirmed and clawed at the opening, his tail thrashing in frustration like a snake on fire. What he wouldn't give to have earth powers at this moment…

As soon as that thought entered his mind, the ground began to rumble. "Wait! I was kidding! I don't want them!" And the crevice ripped open as a large rock booted him out, the poor purple beast yelping as he flipped through the air and landed flat on his back with a hiss. He opened one eye when he heard a chuckle and looked up. A forest green dragon with grey eyes and a whip-like tail was standing over him, seeming highly amused.

"Not a word, Marshall." He smacked the larger dragon with his wing, rolling over and rising to his feet. This was embarrassing enough without commentary.

Marshall shook his head, suddenly becoming serious.

"Did you do it?"

"No faith… I am surprised at you, my dear, green friend."

"Scream, did you or did you not complete the task?"

Usually Marshall was all for the 'less-experienced dragon's playfulness,' as Marshall so lovingly put it. That is what finally made the purple terror relent. "Yes. Though whether it succeeded is another question entirely."

"That will have to suffice. We need to head back. Krohn can't hold his own for much longer."

That is when Scream lost it. "You left that old geezer alone to fight the monsters?!" Marshall only rolled his eyes and took to the skies, Scream ranting right behind him as they made their not-so-long flight back to the ruins.

The ruins weren't much, hence the name "ruins." However, the maze-like structure and strategically placed decaying towers were perfect for defense and getting your enemies terribly lost. Well, it had been great for that, until the nasty little goblins had blown a hole straight through the wall, letting in all sorts of vile creatures to blow up more of the already crumbling walls. Scream thought it was quite the… interesting scene.

Marshall rolled his body up as he glowed a lime green, encasing himself in rock and plummeting from the sky. He smashed down and rolled across the floor, taking down any who got in his way.

Scream had no time to envy the wrecking ball of a dragon; the winged vipers were back on his tail, though this time he didn't have a mission hindering him. He grinned as he charged them, beating his wings faster and tackling them out of the sky head-on. "Tag! You're it!" They plummeted with him like stones, screeching and snapping at him. He swiped both of their faces with his claws and quickly pulled away as the snakes crashed to the floor, Scream flying off.

"Maniac," Marshall grumbled, his tail smacking down a few goblins. "Scream, go find Krohn! Now!" The smaller dragon saluted before soaring over the ruins, searching for the withered old lizard. When Scream was last with Krohn, he had set Scream on a mission and told him to only come back when he had completed it. "Maybe he's waiting for me to come back to the pools…" Immediately he made his decision and veered left, heading for the water. If he was still there, he would need backup; that dragon could barely see at his age.

"Ah. There they are." He dove down as soon as he saw the hatching pools glinting in the setting sun, frowning when he noticed the strange colors painting them and the murky ground. He landed by all the pools and froze, his red eyes wide. In every pool and nest were smashed eggshells and yolks spilling out the sides. There was goo and blood everywhere. He resisted the urge to vomit and began to slink forward with his head low. "K-Krohn...?" He wasn't sure whether he expected a response or not, nor was he sure he even wanted one. "Krohn, are you here...?" How could he let this happen?

Scream almost jumped as he suddenly heard a scraping sound below. He lifted his paw and shuddered as he flicked shell pieces off his talons. He was getting really freaked out and sick to his stomach. "I can't believe I'm even seeing this... this is a low blow..." he muttered, right before pausing in his tracks. Something glinted in the fading light beneath a pile of crackling hay.

A thin screen of smoke mostly hid the object from view, but the smoke was fading in the evening breeze. He slowly moved towards it, claws gently scraping the dirt as his tail swayed from side to side, curiosity lighting up his eyes. Could it be…?

It was. A shiny, black, round surface with red spots hidden in the smoke, looking exactly like a miracle in the middle of the debris of carnage. Scream's talons slowly encased the delicate egg, lifting it out of the hay and examining it with a small smile. "Well, look at you, little one. Quite the scrapper." It was probably because of Krohn that this egg had even managed to survive; Krohn was definitely talented at smokescreens. However, his absence also testified of either his capture or worse. "Looks like we just have to head back to Marshall without him. He's going to chew my hide…"

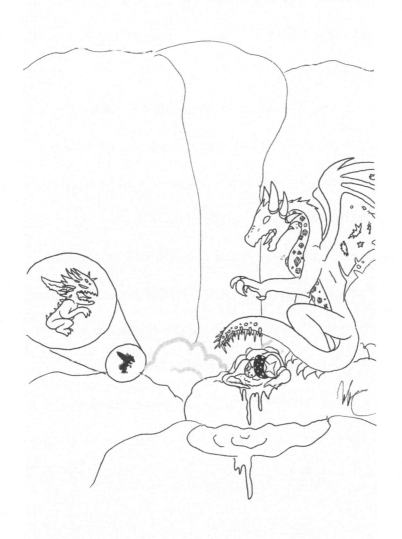

CRACK!

~????~

It was the first thing I heard. I didn't quite know what I was seeing. It was... dim, not really dark. Something was glowing, and I wanted to know what it was. I moved, but my head hit something. So, it was going to be like that. Very well, then. I kept bumping my head against whatever had me ensnared. It was a dumb struggle, looking back on this. Finally, the barrier broke, and I tumbled out, yelping as my body flew over my head repeatedly.

I slowly opened my eyes to see where I was, and why everything was so dark, unlike the inside of wherever I had been before. There were pieces of glowing... something all around me, a nasty goo all over me. I made a face as I shook it off, then made a strained effort to stand. My legs were wobbly and almost refused to hold up my body, but after a long while of perseverance, I could stand.

I grinned, then squeaked in surprise and a little fear as something started flapping behind me. I tumbled headfirst as I tried to escape from the terrifying noise, scrambling for my life... and tumbling outside the mouth of the cave. I barely slid to a stop in time, half of my body hanging over the edge of a small cliff. My little claws scraped the side of the cliff for any hold they could catch, but I had just learned how to stand; I hadn't learned anything else yet. This learning was slow going.

Finally, my dumb claws curled around a rock, and my leg was able to push me back up over the edge. That had been too close for comfort. I had to figure out my body before I could do anything else. But first things first: I had to find the freaky noise. I crawled forward with a lot of difficulty, looking around the cave. There it was again! I looked up towards the noise and squeaked. Large, orange, feather things were stuck in my back!

It took me a moment to realize that the orange things were part of me; they fluttered and flapped when I wanted them to and it hurt to bite them. So, they were mine. I looked down at my clawed toes and wiggled them. They were also mine. A stubby, feathery tail thrashed. Yes, that was also mine. I gave a toothy grin and giggled, bouncing around and falling over, scrambling back to my feet. My orange feather flappers helped me stand as I beat them furiously. Okay.

Now that I was back on my feet, I could examine myself to better understand what I was. Hopefully.

I glanced down at my toes again. Long golden claws protruded from them. My scaly toes and legs were a bright aquamarine color and seemed to glow just like the icky goo-mess I came out of. My plated underbelly was gold just like my claws, same as my feathery fluff on the end of my aquamarine tail. My orange flappers had a gold frame with a little claw on the arch. That was all I could see of me.

All in all, I decided I looked pretty cool. The only problem was... what the heck was I?

I looked around for any answer, but there was nobody else in sight. At that moment, I realized how incredibly lonely I was starting to feel. Maybe there were others outside that could help. I scrambled to the opening and frantically beat my flappers, squeaking when I lifted into the air, wobbling toward the bottom of the cliffside. I could fly?! This was going to be easier than walking. Though, as I scanned the area, I realized that flying would probably have the same results as walking.

All I could find in my line of sight was cracked, dead ground. There was absolutely nothing to see. My eyes were wide as I flew (if you could call it flying) over the land, searching for a sign of anything other than rock and wasteland. I beat my flappers harder and slower to lift myself higher, landing on top of the cliff, above the little cave I now called home. Maybe I could see better from up here. But it had the same results; my flappers fell as I sighed, concluding that nobody else was here and I was alone.

This strange feeling started building up inside me and I couldn't calm it; I didn't even know what it was. It just kept building up and overwhelming me, my scales glowing brighter and brighter. I thought I was going to pop. Fortunately, it was just this blue glowing stuff leaking out of my body and mouth and blinding me. Unfortunately, it was THIS BLUE GLOWING STUFF LEAKING OUT OF MY BODY AND BLINDING ME! I started screaming in terror, frustration, sorrow -- but mostly terror, which turned into this strange roar as it grew brighter, forcing me to shut my eyes to avoid going permanently blind.

It felt like forever until the feeling left and it was dark behind my eyelids again. Slowly and warily I opened my eyes. And then it felt like I couldn't breathe. There was this… lush, green, fluffy stuff on the ground, torrents of bright shining blue rushing down from what used to be large cracks in the dirt. Tall brown giants with green fluffy tops filtered light through them, touching the sky and planting their long bodies in the dirt, huddled together like a pack.

Only their fluffy tops seemed to move, swaying back and forth. I looked down at my cave to see the shining blue falling from the cliff, only the ledge of the cave still visible as it poked out from the tumbling blue. I fluttered to the ledge and made a very undignified landing attempt. In other words, I flew and tumbled through the crashing blue -- which was freezing -- and rolled to a stop in the middle of the small cave.

I squirmed back to my feet, puzzling over what had just happened. Where had all this strange color come from? How did it get here? I decided I no longer cared. I was going to go enjoy it. It was so… pretty. So, so pretty. I wandered back to the mouth of the cave, the blue splashing as it hit the edge. I ran straight through it, squeaking as it soaked me from head to tail, my flappers beating themselves dry. I did this a couple more times, laughing and squealing before I fluttered to the top of the cliff again.

A large body of blue was crashing against the dirt and pouring down the cliff in front of my cave, emptying into the cracks and flowing in different directions through the area; I had my own little… paradise. Yes, that was the word. I was so filled with joy and excitement that I wanted badly to share this. But there was still no one. My eyes started leaking suddenly as my tail hid between my legs and my flappers tucked against my spiky back. How did I make it stop leaking? Were my eyes melting?! I couldn't get them to stop no matter how hard I tried. So, I just let it happen; if it killed me, so be it.

My body was shaking, and these pitiful noises were escaping my snout. I let out another roar, sparking flashes of blue bolting from my mouth and lighting up the sky for a small moment before vanishing like they were never there.

I curled up on the bluff and decided sleep would make all these terrible churning feelings go away. I was tired anyway, and my tummy was making these weird gurgling noises, but I didn't know what to eat. Sleep might also help me ignore my dumb tummy. I dove back into my cave and curled around a rock, closing my eyes and hoping for peaceful sleep.

STIRRINGS

~????~

For many nights, at first, it was complete and total darkness, which was actually kind of peaceful for a moment but then became very unsettling. Suddenly a bright light chased the darkness away. When the light cleared, I saw large, flying, horned beasts that looked similar to me, trapped in dark barriers and frozen in place with red fog that took on the appearance of chains. Their eyes were wide but looked like they were staring at nothing. What could they possibly be seeing to cause such mighty, powerful creatures to tremble and stare endlessly in terror? Each of them had a name that appeared in my head as I faced them: Marshall was the green one, the ground shaking below him; BogMire was the two-headed red one, dripping with flames; and Krohn was the withered yellow one, standing tall as smoke billowed from his snout. Krohn looked determined to stay standing, even though the chains were sapping his energy. However, he couldn't last much longer; he was old and tired.

As I reached out to him, another bright light blinded me. My flappers shielded my eyes. I then saw a purple creature, spikier than the others, with sparkly rocks stuck in his soft underbelly. He wasn't imprisoned like the others; he was curled up in some distant place, in hiding with his many injuries. It was probably a smart move, considering the fates of the others. His name came to me as well: Scream. There was an indescribable feeling as I looked at him and thought of his name. It was... sort of warm. And fuzzy. I didn't know what it was at the time, but I wanted to see him.

I watched him as he lifted his head to let out a loud cry of mourning, "SYRYNN!" His call startled me awake. So that was my name; he knew my name and my mind knew it was mine, just as it had known the other names. It was way better than Rock Queen, queen of many rocks, which I had taken to calling myself. What else was I supposed to be called when I had no name? But even though the question of what to call me had been answered, I now had more questions than ever. What was I and what were they? Was this dream even real? Why did I know who they were? Why did I connect to Scream so strongly and how did he know my name? Who were they? Why was he calling for me?

Where was he? Where were the others and why were they being tortured?

Why was I here?

This made me realize that I really didn't have a clue what was going on. However, rather than dwell on it, which wouldn't do me any good anyway since I didn't know what to do, I flew out to explore and hopefully feed myself. My tummy was killing me.

DARK SHADOW

~SHADOW~

I couldn't remember anything from my past -- not that I had much of one. Every time I tried to recall it, my mind would cloud over, and I'd be sitting like a mindless zombie for a couple of hours. So, I relented and concluded that it was not important enough for me to risk my mind; I had more important things to focus on.

Judging from my current status, I assumed my master had always been my master. He wouldn't make just anyone his number two. That's what he told me anyway, and why would I question him? Why would he lie to me, his faithful right-hand dragon?

One thing did bother me, though. I did ask him why I didn't remember anything before our last battle, and he told me when the evil dragons attacked and wounded me, my memories were lost, so my master had to "upgrade" me to fend them off. He was proud of me for capturing two of the evil dragons as soon as his magic made me bigger and stronger, but he was disappointed that I had let one important one escape. My new mission was Scream; I was to find him and take him down, bring him back, and put him with the other prisoners so we could drain their energy and free the being that Master called Strife. We had to open a portal using the dragons' energies that Master had collected over time. He just needed one more.

He wouldn't tell me why we were freeing this "Strife" guy, but I wasn't one to question his motives. Well... mostly. I knew he valued blind obedience and hated to be questioned, but sometimes I couldn't help it. "Is this the right thing to do?"

His growl was vicious and deep, his black scales rattling like a snake. "It's the only thing to do, you little-!" He pounded his paw into the floor, cracking the stone as he bellowed, "IF WE DON'T, THERE WILL BE NO PEACE AND EVIL DRAGONS WILL DESTROY US ALL!"

I shrank away in fear; he'd never shown so much anger at me before, nor had he ever bared his teeth at me like this. His growl became softer, "Shadow... it's because of me that you're alive. All I ask is that you trust me. I took you in and made you stronger. You'd still be a whimpering whelp and easy prey for those terrible monsters that call themselves dragons. I would never lead you astray."

I slowly nodded, my fear ebbing away.

"Good. Good." He straightened up and jerked his head to the exit. "Now go find Scream and bring him here. I'll make sure he regrets ever betraying me. Once you bring him back, we'll be able to get him to tell us where he hid that egg. That hatchling could very well be our downfall if it lives. If you find it on your mission, kill it."

I bowed my head to him and half-whispered, "Yes, Master." I now unwillingly left his lair and took off into the night to search the skies. I never intended to kill a child. I still felt like one myself; it was only because of my master's influence that I was as big and strong as a fully-grown dragon. I didn't want to find this hatchling; I hoped I wouldn't come across it.

The more I dwelt on this, the more I realized I didn't

want to torture these dragons either. I mean, aren't we all dragons? However, orders were orders, and we had to do what we had to do to keep the world safe from the evils of our kind. So... why did I feel so guilty about doing it? I shook it off; petty feelings of weakness would not stop my mission or cause me to falter. We were doing the right thing in keeping our world safe from corrupted dragons. If we didn't stop them, they would wreak all sorts of havoc.

    Feeling better about my mission and back in the right state of mind, I climbed higher and higher into the sky.

SCREAM'S NOT HOME RIGHT NOW

~SCREAM~

I groaned as I opened my eyes, entirely sore and not really wanting to get up but knowing I had to. I wasn't safe. Shadow would come back for me if I didn't move right now. I reluctantly rose to my feet and shook the mud from my scales. It had served its purpose of hiding a bright purple dragon in the swamp. I pondered how I was going to leave the swamp without being detected, especially in broad daylight while being hunted by a dragon whose element was the literal darkness. So that meant no hiding in the dark either. I didn't want the shade suddenly swallowing me up like it did Marshall. That had been a terrifying event to watch.

Suddenly, I remembered the egg and felt sick to my stomach. I was told to hide it and I had hidden it in the most desolate place on the planet. In the moment, it had seemed genius; nobody would think to look there for it. But I had neglected the fact that nobody would think to look for it there because no egg could survive there. I was an idiot. An idiot and a failure. Why didn't that thought occur to me before I had thrown the egg in that cave and flew away? Was I really that dense?!

Marshall would be so disappointed in me. It was a wonder he even let me be his apprentice at the hatchery as a caretaker when I couldn't even get basic egg survival down.

No wonder they still didn't trust me; I had killed their last hope.

However, as I was about to lie back down in my shame and guilt, something told me that it wouldn't hurt to check. If it was still alive, then it would be a pleasant surprise. If it wasn't alive, then it would confirm my fears, and nothing would change. I didn't have much else to lose, nor could I do anything else. I'd need help freeing my friends, which I couldn't very well attempt on my own; I'd already lost.

I spread my wings wide and took to the skies before Shadow even showed up, making sure to stay low so I'd be harder to spot. My wings beat in a steady rhythm, carrying me through the shady swamps and across the land in little to no time at all.

I immediately pulled my wings back like a parachute to stop myself as I stared in shock, my wings beating but keeping me suspended in place, not entirely certain I was seeing this correctly. This place had been a desert for decades, but at this very moment it was teeming with plant life and river rapids flowed through it. I almost didn't recognize it. In fact, the only reason I did was because this was the exact location and those rivers were right where those craggy canyons used to be. What in the world had happened here? How did this paradise even come to exist, especially in such a short amount of time? Wait... was the egg still even here? My heart jumped into my throat as I dove into the cave built into the cliffside, crashing through the water, and shaking myself dry. I frantically scanned the cave. Where was it, where was it?

I slowed to a stop at the back of the cave, behind a rock formation, my heart sinking all the way down to my talons, agonizingly slow; there was nothing. Nothing but glowing blue pieces of shell and neon goo splattered all over. So, they actually found it. My head lowered to the floor as I forlornly nudged a piece.

"What are you doing here?" A small terrified voice squeaked behind me. I nearly jumped out of my scales and spun around to see an aquamarine hatchling standing in the mouth of the cave, with golden spiraling horns, bright icy green eyes, a golden star crest on her forehead, and spikes running down from the top of her head to the tip of her tail, which ended in feathery fluff. She glowed as brilliant as a warm fire on a cold night, and boy, was I glad to see that little scowling face.

She was obviously frightened of the much larger stranger in her home, so I decided to take it slow, considering this prophecy dragon had just created an entire oasis in the short time that I was gone. I was going to start with the basics. And tell her everything.

As only a good guardian would do.

INTRUDER

~SYRYNN~

I became curious as I stared at this purple creature that looked like me. Maybe he knew what I was and could tell me. Maybe it was a bad thing if he knew. He could be dangerous. I took a small step back just in case, but I was surprised when he took a step forward and smiled at me. That could either be a happy-to-see-me smile... or a this-is-a-nice-appetizer-I-have-found smile. I was getting uneasy. I may not have known him, but he definitely knew me.

As I started to dash to the opening of the cave, his spiked tail flew up and smacked against the ceiling. A crack grew and split the rock until my exit caved in, pebbles raining down around the boulders. I swallowed hard. This guy was terrifying. I turned back around, slowly backing up against the cave-in. He took steps towards me, causing me to tense up and get ready to, um, light him up with... er... something that would be painful. I was so dead. But I was ready to go down fighting if he came too close.

He chuckled, his voice a calm whisper, "You don't have to be like that, you know." I uncoiled myself but still remained on high alert. When he came closer, I tensed again, and he had the nerve to laugh. "I don't mean you any harm, hatchling." Hatchling? Was that what I was? "You must be very confused and frightened, but Syrynn, you're safe now. And I will tell you everything you need to know." He knew *the* name-- My name! And then it came crashing down, hitting me hard; he was the purple creature from my dream that had called out my name. Almost immediately, I became calm. I was okay. He was friendly.

He stretched out until he slumped onto the floor, tail curling around his legs and making himself comfortable. "All right. First things first, you're an exceptional little aquamarine dragon who has a rare and extraordinary ability. And your destiny is to stop evil dragons from blowing our planet to smithereens." I stared blankly into his eyes. What was he spewing?

"Could you, ah… maybe slow it down a bit? I don't know what you're talking about."

"Right." He looked flustered. "Sorry. I was a bad choice for all this helpful junk." He then cleared his throat before starting again. "So, there's this war that started up between dragons. Typical good guys versus bad guys. The good guys defeated the bad guys -- or guy in this case -- and now he's back, that sort of deal. I won't quite go into details; it's pretty grisly, so let's talk more about your role in all this. Because of this war, the dragon species is near extinct, really. Every time the dragon population dwindles, a certain dragon is born to fix that. Kind of like a queen bee if you will. She oversees replenishing the species, but unfortunately this bad dragon that has come back sees you- well more particularly your gift as a threat, mostly since you were not born on his side of the war."

I tilted my head, puzzled. "Queen bee?"

"You'll have to ask Krohn more about that one. He's lived long enough to see another of you. Probably. Look, I'm not very good at all this. All I know is that this dragon has the power to create. I have no idea the limits of this power and neither does your newfound enemy. He was quite livid when he heard the news that your egg showed up in our care. He sent his armies of creatures to destroy it. Fortunately, we all pitched in so I could get you to safety. Unfortunately, the other dragons I worked with are now captured, and who knows what that undead freak is doing to them." He then sighed. "Sorry, I got a bit carried away there. I'm still a little miffed. Anyway, because of all this, I need your help."

This sounded entirely insane. He expected me to do something like that? This was all outside of my capabilities. As he explained more about this war and the task I was given before birth, I became even more certain that I could not do it, even if we were up against some spirit dragon that had died a long time ago at the claws of Scream. How was I supposed to stop a dead dragon?

He tried to comfort me. "I know, I know. It's a lot to take in. Don't worry, little one. Your gift will help you. But use it only when you really need to; something like that is sure to demand a lot of magic, and a large loss of magic takes a long time to recover. Your little body can't handle using it willy nilly just yet." How was I supposed to use said gift if I didn't even know what it was, or how I apparently used it in the first place? What was he talking about? What was this ability and why wasn't he elaborating? I wanted to scream at Scream. That sounded like it would help my frustration. Maybe that was why they called him Scream. I brought this to his attention, and he chuckled. "Surely you noticed the wasteland outside that is no longer a wasteland. I'm assuming that was you. After all, no other dragon on this entire planet is capable of creating something out of nothing. Nobody else can tell you how to work it but you."

Well, that was disappointing. I still didn't know how to use it. "If I don't know how to use my ability yet... then what can I use to help me?"

"Well, judging from your body type and color, I'm going to assume your natural elemental powers are ice and electricity. Every dragon has elemental powers. You do know how to use those, yes?" I thought back to the blue sparks that left my mouth the other day and assumed that's what he was talking about. I nodded. I knew how to do that. That came easy. "Good," He continued, "And keep this in mind: You aren't safe in the sky. A black dragon named Shadow wants to kill you and take me as a prisoner. Stay on the ground for now." I nodded in understanding. Avoiding the evil dragons sounded like a good plan.

Then he said something that startled me. "You are also going to free the guardian dragons. It shouldn't be too hard for someone your size, neither will they be expecting you. You can slip right in and free them, and then they can assist you in helping them escape. Krohn is the closest. He's north of here in Pyreworks. You'll know the place when you see it."

I immediately protested as he told me where to go. "Why don't you do it?" He was a lot stronger and obviously knew what he was doing more than I ever could. Scream chuckled. "Because I'm too big, my dear, and can't possibly sneak in. They'd catch me and torture me to death. You, on the other hand, could slip right through the cracks of the rock walls and break the dragons out. Just use your size to your advantage. I have to go now; I can't stay in one place for too long or Shadow will find me. I have faith in you and wish you all the luck in the world." He then smashed his head through the pile of rocks, all of them giving way to the force and tumbling down the cliff, splashing into the water below. He spread his torn, red wings wide.

"Wait! What do I do then?" I called after him, trying to run to catch up.

He grinned over his shoulder at me. "Come to the ruins. Krohn will lead you there." And with that, he flew off, leaving me standing there on the ledge. I huffed and decided to go back to bed; I was going to need all the strength I could gather for tomorrow. If Krohn was anything like Scream, I was going to throw a fit.

THE HUNT IS ON

~SHADOW~

I had been searching for days trying to find Scream. At least there was still no sign of the egg, or a hatchling. That was a small relief. I wanted to put that off as long as I could. However, this search was growing tiresome and my patience was growing thin. I made a quick stop to slash open a jungle cat and swallow it whole. There. That felt much better. I took off again and searched harder and checked every nook and cranny of every biome near me. Nothing. No Scream. No egg.

Frustration was building. I was getting terribly irritated with these negative results. I needed to find the wretched purple dragon in order to complete my quest. The days seemed to grow longer and longer as I searched to no avail. How hard could it be to find a bright purple dragon covered in spikes? Apparently pretty, stupidly hard.

As I flew, I idly began to rethink what my master had said about the hatchling, his words echoing in my head: "It could destroy us if it lives." I almost scoffed at this warning. How could it achieve such a feat? It was only a child.

Then my mind began to doubt; maybe it had some secret power that could. This dumb thought started to plague my mind with growing fear. Maybe it could destroy me, and I was being too arrogant. I had to find Scream fast. If I could catch him before I even saw the child, they wouldn't be able to stop the plan in time. The three dragons we already had didn't have enough power without Scream. So long as that purple menace ran free, I would not succeed. Master hated failure. I kept up my tireless search, knowing he had to eventually show up. He couldn't hide from me forever.

ALMOST UNWANTED GUEST

~SCREAM~

I was exhausted from all my flying and hiding and anxiety of getting caught or losing Syrynn. I should have gone with her. No. I was just as bad as a beacon pointing exactly where to get hatchling hash. I made it too risky. She would have to do it alone.

I landed in front of a cave in the deep reaches of

the swamp to rest awhile, when I paused as my ear picked up what sounded like whimpering inside. Against my better judgement, I decided to go check it out. Whatever was whimpering couldn't be dangerous. Usually.

    I slowly crept inside, low to the floor as I scanned the interior of the cave. At first, I couldn't really see anything in the darkness, but the deeper I traveled, the more I noticed a strange orange glow that appeared as if something was attempting to smother it. As any curious reptile would do, I ventured even further inside, towards the glow.

    A black mist became visible, so thick I could hardly move through it, slowly hiding the orange light from view. I strained against the dense, dark fog until I suddenly fell through it, tumbling into a large chamber and coming to a stop in front of three dragons. Well, one was a dragon and two were hatchlings, a little older than Syrynn and Shadow. Obviously, they were neutral dragons because I had never seen their faces before; neutral dragons tended to remain in hiding away from everyone else while the dragons who took a side to this war remained available to go to battle.

The dragon approached me, her scales the soft orange of flower petals, her claws, wing membrane, eyes, and curved horns a light green. She wore a silver collar around her neck, her plated underbelly a darker shade of green, black speckles spotting her shoulders and cheeks. Her colors were quite the contrast. She stood in front of the young ones, hissing at me as the wind picked up around her. "If you value your life, leave now." The hatchlings must have been hers. It was unwise to stand between a mother and her younglings. But I just couldn't help but stare; wind dragons were so uncommon, and I had just happened upon one.

The babies looked up at me with large doleful eyes, the male a red fire dragon with a flame dancing on the end of his tail. The female was the first white dragon I had ever seen. She was ghostly white, shadowy mist billowing off the tip of her tail. I didn't quite notice something else was odd until I saw their mouthless snouts. The twins didn't have a mouth. How did they even speak? Or eat, for that matter?

I heard their mother growl again, pulling me out of my thoughts. "Did you not hear me? I told you to leave!"

I backed up slowly, lowering myself into a submissive position. "I didn't come to harm you. I was only looking for a place to stay."

Her growling slowly ceased. Surprised at my willing submission, she rose from her tensed position and studied me.

"Well… you don't look entirely like a threat. Suppose you can stay." She pointed the leaf on the end of her tail to the red child. "That's Pyre." Her tail moved to the white one. "And that's Nyxx." Her tail fell back behind her. "I'm Ivy. What about you?"

"Scream."

"What?"

"My name is Scream. That wasn't a command, I swear."

She only smirked at that. Pyre and Nyxx had already passed out in a pile of swamp plants. That didn't take very long. Nyxx's tail twitched every so often, Pyre's body squishing her against the floor, both of them looking pretty happy, nonetheless.

She gave me a droll stare as I watched her dragonlings, and then answered the question that I had left hanging in the air. "I dunno why they don't have mouths. Maybe they were born..." I could tell it was a sore topic, but she continued anyway, "With some sort of birth defect. But they communicate telepathically and read the current thoughts of others."

"Seriously?"

"Mmhmm. I haven't quite figured out how they absorb their food, but they do. I've never quite had to deal with this before." She shook her head. "Anyway, I need to get some sleep. We've been on high alert all day. Dangerous area." And with that, she walked back over to her hatchlings, lay down and curled around them, then slowly dozed off. I sauntered over to a corner near the entrance and lightly slept. Someone had to guard the cave.

Now if only I could get over those terrible feelings and nightmares and actually sleep…

CAVE OF NOT SO MUCH WONDER

~SYRYNN~

I was getting close to Krohn's prison, seated right at the deep ends of a forest of fire. The flames licked at the trees, but they never seemed to burn down. I thought I was going to catch heat stroke. I practically crawled my way to the stone walls and flew over them, landing and keeping my head down as I snuck over to the large rocky structure. I was feeling very uneasy and quite thirsty. I squirmed in between a space where a stone had strangely been removed. I found out why almost instantly.

These little nasty creatures with spaded tails and red skin had snuck in and were trying to raid the food and annoy bigger and meaner cow-headed beasties. They were being pests and pulling on the bigger beasts' ears and tails, sometimes even going as far as to tug on the nose ring of one. That actually made the cow man eat the pest right then and there, sending the rest of the little imps into a fit.

While they were distracted with... smaller problems, I headed down a different hall away from them in the hopes of avoiding detection. I kept slipping in through small holes in the walls of this interesting cave that the bigger creatures probably couldn't see or really care about. Scream was right; they really weren't expecting someone like me.

I slid to a stop right in front of a giant cage. A very large, yellow dragon was hanging from these chains made of pure electricity and thrashing as he nonstop roared and roared. There was pain in his wavering voice, so much pain it hurt to listen. But how was I supposed to get him out?

I finally cried out with him, the strange feeling coming back as the same blue energy poured out of me and became a glowing blue ball of light. It slowly changed to yellow and changed shape, looking like an outline of me. The glow around the shape faded and, standing in its place, was a little yellow dragon with a deep red underbelly. She had spikes all over her head and her blue eyes were sparking like lightning, her little legs jogging in place. She looked like a yellow, spiky, hyperactive version of me.

"Uh... Okay... Fizz."

She grinned, tail thrashing. "Yes, that is now me! What are we doing?"

I smirked, then looked up at the cage. "We're going to free Krohn. Any ideas?" She looked up to where I was looking and suggested we absorb the electricity. She was a pretty smart dragon; I was disappointed in myself for not thinking of that earlier. We both opened our mouths and used our electricity powers to begin to absorb the electric chains wrapped around the old dragon. It was definitely a lot easier and faster with two.

We were almost done when he suddenly stiffened, his eyes wild. "RUN! RUN RUN RUN RUN RUN!" He thrashed in the remaining two chains, while both of us backed up in terror and confusion, frantically looking around. We froze as an enormous shadow streaked across the ground, circling around Fizz. A purple haze spun around her and hid her from view, but I could see her... changing.

Her eyes glowed red through the fog, her body growing taller and taller until she was as big as Krohn. She slowly turned towards me and lunged out of the haze at me, claws outstretched. I quickly scrambled away and ducked as lightning zipped over my head. I was confused as to why she had changed and was now attacking me. I would have to attack back to save Krohn and survive. I waited for Fizz to charge me again, reared back on my hind legs, and fired a shard of ice out of my mouth at her stomach. It sunk deep into the chink in her plated underbelly, causing her to let out a loud screech and retreat, flying away.

I almost flew after her until remembering I still had to free Krohn. I doubled back and absorbed the last of the chains. The cage then burst apart once he was free, the poor dragon staggering and wheezing. "M-many thanks, little one... we must move before... worse things happen."

He grabbed the cage with his teeth and tossed it in the air, breaking open the ceiling and causing monsters to swarm in from the halls. He grabbed my tail with his teeth before I could react and spread his wings wide, shooting out of the top of the cave and flying off with me in his grip.

Two near heart attacks in one week. I was on a roll.

THE SHADOWS GROW

~SHADOW~

I was feeling quite satisfied with myself. I may have lost the old geezer, but I already succeeded in draining what I needed, and as a bonus, I had gained a new little companion. Evidently her name was Fizz, and she was going to be helping me with my mission from now on. It seemed that the egg had hatched and now I would have to dispose of it. But now, I didn't directly have to be involved. I could just go send Fizz to do it. How sad to be destroyed by your own creation.

The plan was coming along nicely, even if I hadn't caught Scream yet. The hatchling had only succeeded in removing a worn-out piece that was in need of being thrown away anyway. I was surprised we even got that much power out of those withered, ancient bones.

I guided Fizz to my lair and began to devise a new plan to stay ahead of the little blue monstrosity and lure Scream in to make my job easier.

SCREAM OF THE ANXIOUS
~SCREAM~

I hated not knowing anything. Don't scream, don't scream, don't scream. I paced the floor back and forth and back and forth, chewing on the inside of my cheek. Ghastly little habit of anxiety. It had been a few hours since I left the cave. I scanned the ruins, anxiously watching. Panic wasn't very becoming of me, but I couldn't help it. Where were

Krohn and Syrynn?

The more I waited, the more I regretted my rash decision of hinting at what she was and throwing her out into enemy territory. I was a little too excited; I'll admit that. I should have at least spent a little more time explaining things. I just hoped my shortcomings weren't the untimely death of our only hope. That would mean I had ultimately failed yet again, and I did not think I could live with that.

Then, I heard a loud thud behind me, the ground shaking at some sort of harsh impact. Only one dragon in the world landed that heavily. I was surprised he had never broken his legs doing that. I found myself dashing to them as fast as I could, grinning. "SYRYNN!"

FAMILY REUNION

~SYRYNN~

"Scream!" I wriggled out of Krohn's mouth and scrambled to meet him. "I did it, I did it!" I squealed.

Scream laughed and nuzzled my snout with his. "You did wonderful. I told you so."

I grinned wide, then yelped as two blurs whizzed by me. I started to give chase, but my legs were running in place. I looked back as Scream let go of my tail. "Don't worry, they're friendly. I'm sure you'll be great friends with Pyre and Nyxx. Ah… which reminds me."

Scream bonked Krohn on the head with his spiky tail. "You little sneak!"

Krohn hissed, rubbing his head ruefully with his wing. "What? What did I do?"

I watched in confusion as Scream dragged Krohn away by the ear. I ran after them to keep up. Where were they going?

THE OTHER, OTHER HATCHLING

~????~

I heard voices. Which was nothing new, I heard them all the time, but it still got me curious; they were headed my way. I should have been scared like a normal, well… whatever I was. But instead, I snuck towards them, which wasn't easy. I tripped over my own enormous feet with every step and tasted dirt. So, I just decided to stay put and have a look at myself since I couldn't go anywhere anyway.

Lime green scales, golden claws and golden rock-hard belly to match, orange flappy things lined with gold, stumpy tail with golden feather fluffy nonsense at the end, and light blue bubbly designs starting at my claws and ending below the joints of all my legs.

"I swear, I can explain."

I squeaked and leapt to my feet. Three… whatever they were… stared right at me, the yellow one looking kinda sheepish. I liked sheep. The blue one tilted her head. "You found another one? I thought you said all the eggs were smashed."

The purple one sighed. "That's what I thought. Apparently Krohn hid a good portion of the eggs away." He glanced at the yellow one. "You made me think I got them all smashed, you jerk."

Yellow Scaly protested, "I couldn't carry them all

and couldn't alert the monsters that I had succeeded in hiding some. That meant leaving no hint for you, either. I knew you'd find them though if that makes you feel better."

"Marshall beat my hide!"

"Ah yes, that was to keep it authentic. Couldn't tell either of you for fear of the monsters catching word that there was a batch they missed."

"Well… I… guess that makes sense…"

The blue one seemed to be studying me, both of the bigger ones looking at her to see her reaction. She then sat down. "It's cute." They both seemed to look rather disappointed, as if they were expecting something more from her.

Purple Scaly sighed in defeat, then smirked. "I guess he is." I beamed, my tail thrashing. He turned back to Blue Scaly. "He needs a name. You want to choose one?" Ooh! I was getting a name! I squirmed in place.

She looked me over, biting her lip. "Uhmmm… Spyr?" She gave a helpless shrug. Purple Scaly smiled and nodded his approval. I liked it too. Nice ring to it. Like the voices in my ears.

"Well, Spyr. My name is Scream, and this is Syrynn and Krohn. Welcome to the ruins." I grinned at all of them. We were going to have so much fun. The voices told.

ROLLING STONE

~SHADOW~

"SOUND THE ALARM!"

I groaned. This was great. Just what I needed. Stress. I trudged out of my chamber to see goblins scrambling around in a state of panic. I threw my head back and roared to get their attention. All of them froze as I stalked over to one. "What now?" I demanded.

"M-Marshall, sir. He's escaping."

"HOW?!" I shrieked.

The goblin shrank to the ground in fear. "A... a sort of... blue dragon and her companion have broken his prison free and are tumbling it... down the hills." He gulped.

I roared in fury and flew to his icy prison. How did they even get in? Was everyone here as thick as boulders?! I paused mid-flight as I watched an interesting spectacle: the earth dragon's cell of ice was rolling down the hills and painting the hills red with goblin goo, minotaur brains, and snake scales, the two little dragons running behind it. One was the blue hatchling from before and the other was a slightly bigger and very faded purple dragon with dark purple horns and pink designs. I sneered. They were both easy targets from behind. I noticed Fizz awaiting my command nearby, just out of the hatchling's sight. I nodded, then breathed out a black mist, encasing this new dragon the hatchling had brought with her.

"Misty!" the hatchling shrieked, dashing towards her, but was then cut off by Fizz, forcing her to run the other way and dodge a volley of lightning bolts. I watched the battle, though I kept my eye on this Misty dragon. She seemed to be another one of those pathetic little creations of the hatchling.

She was a little bigger than Fizz had been and a little more mature. But she still succumbed to the darkness. Her dark purple eyes became red, just like mine and Fizz's. She grew to our size and let out a loud roar, spitting a purple fluid, and splashing the hatchling in the face. She screamed in agony, backing up and trying to wipe it away with her wings. I could hear the sizzling from here. Poison was very unpleasant.

At that moment, the block of ice hit the gate and shattered to pieces. Marshall thrashed as he sprang to his feet, rearing back and slamming his paws on the ground. Jagged rocks shot out of the ground right underneath both Fizz and Misty, launching them up into the air. No, no, no, no, no!

Marshall's eyes glowed as rock encased the hatchling and rolled down the hill towards him. He then cracked it open with his head and picked her up in his mouth. He spread his wings wide and took off with the hatchling, quickly disappearing from sight. I ground my teeth together in frustration. Until… I realized this may actually turn out in my favor. I may have lost the earth dragon, but I gained another companion and accidentally set a new plan into motion all in one day. However, I still had a feeling that Master wouldn't take this loss lightly… even if I had managed to complete the draining process just in time.

FRIGHT AND FLIGHT

~SCREAM~

I woke up and yawned, stretching like a cat. It had been at least a day since Misty and Syrynn had left to find Marshall, and I was exhausted from dealing with the nightmares of children. Since Krohn had returned, more eggs had started hatching, giving Spyr and the others more friends to play with but creating more monkeys to worry about. Every single one of them seemed to think I was a jungle gym, including Shade and Callie, one purple and one pink, and both dragoness rascals. Always together. Always looking up to the pranksters. At least Spyr kept them busy.

However, the more I was left to my own thoughts, the more I began to worry about Syrynn. They were taking longer than expected; Marshall's prison was out in a frozen wasteland, completely unguarded. Something must have happened. I slowly rose, but I wasn't on my feet for more than two seconds before they were tackled out from under me and my snout pushed against the broken tiled floor. I heard giggling and glanced up. Spyr, Pyre, and Nyxx were on my back, thinking their puny weight could hold me down.

Then I looked into Spyr's baby blue eyes, not exactly liking the strange look he was giving me. He was sort of grinning down at me, his eyes slowly swirling to purple. What in the world…?

And then I couldn't move. I was somehow frozen in place and I couldn't even turn my head. Fear was involuntarily building up inside me. How did this little hatchling have the power of freaking fear?! The little cheater was freezing me with it! So not cool! I mean, I guess it sort of made sense, considering his... you know what, that's not important.

Before I could start to worry about this predicament, the fear suddenly stopped, and I could move again. The hatchlings were taking off towards the ruins' gates. I had a feeling I knew why; it was about time. I smirked and followed their lead. I'd get them back later.

WRECKING CREW
~SYRYNN~

I sulked back to the dragon ruins, feeling very miserable and in pain, though Marshall had used his powers to extract the poison from my face and heal it a little. It had still scarred up, but that wasn't why I was depressed. First Fizz, now Misty. I couldn't even protect my own creations from whatever was happening to them. Was I doing something wrong?

"Cheer up, Syrynn. It's not your fault. Shadow has control over anything that has to do with darkness. Even something as little as doubt or fear can give him a hold on you. Keep your chin up and you're untouchable." Marshall smiled, hoping I would too. I managed one back just to make him happy, though he seemed to know it wasn't genuine.

The gates of the ruins opened up and three dragons rolled out. Scream called out, "Thank the stars you've returned! Take these little monstrosities off my talons; I can't take it any longer!"

Spyr, Pyre, and Nyxx mauled Marshall and I in excitement until Scream pried them off us with great effort. Clingy monkeys.

Then I noticed Scream's eyes were on me, specifically my face, not on the wrigglers in his claws. It took me a moment to realize he was staring at my scars, concern in his gaze. I offered the best reassuring smile I could give him, attempting to convince him that the wounds were not painful. It failed, but he turned his attention back to Spyr, who had escaped and tackled me yet again. What a relief this distraction was.

SPYR IN HER SIDE

~SPYR~

"Take me with youuuuuu!" I pleaded as Scream dragged me off Syrynn for the second time in two minutes. I so badly wanted to be out there, saving the world and stuff. By her side. It would be so cool, like a band of superheroes.

She shook the dirt off her scales. "Well, will you be a nuisance?"

"No!" I crossed my heart with a claw. Her eyes were

on my back legs. I guess she wasn't around to see me learn how to walk. All the others were used to me walking around on my hind legs by now. Even Scream decided to stop being surprised.

To my surprise, she said nothing about it and continued inside. I followed eagerly. She was my big sis, but she didn't know it yet and Scream told me not to tell her. So instead, I was gonna keep her safe and not leave her side.

Marshall glanced around. "Where's Krohn?"

Scream immediately replied, "Sickbay."

Of course, I had to go see why, so I followed them, much to their dismay. Krohn was on the shoreline behind the ruins, sneezing and coughing up a fit, smoke billowing from his nose and mouth as he tried to relax in the ocean water. It would have been funny if he didn't look so terrible.

"Justice's breath, what's wrong with you?"

Krohn spewed ash and smoke, sniffing. "Goblins. Ghastly little creatures give me allergies." Scream and Marshall looked at each other in concern but Krohn waved them off. "There are none in the vicinity. Since our battle anyway. But I still smell their stink. Won't get out of my nose." He sneezed smoke again.

Scream sort of chuckled. "Well, I'll go deal with that. But I was going to go check on the eggs first."

Krohn smirked as Marshall did a double-take. "What eggs?"

"They're all hatched now. Go and see." He had a coughing fit before he pointed to the pools where I had hatched from. Scream and Marshall both walked over and smiled at all the little dragons running around.

Marshall sighed in relief, as if a shroud of darkness was lifted. "Thought they were all smashed…"

"So did I." Scream shook his head. "But we should have known better than to underestimate Krohn."

Ivy was tending to them all and feeding them and whatnot. A small pink hatchling with a heart on the side of her head, and a swirly-horned purple hatchling wandered away from her and sat in front of me. I grinned at them. "Hi, Callie. Hi, Shade."

"Shade!" The purple one giggled, swishing her spaded tail.

The pink one cheered, "Callie!" They responded this way any time their names were said. I found it adorable.

Scream looked to Marshall with a smirk, pointing his tail to Ivy. "Looks like they're already being checked on…" He glanced down to me. "With that being said, it's time you got ready for your mission with Syrynn." I almost heard my heart explode in anticipation. This was my moment.

RIGHT

~SHADOW~

"YOU FOOL!"

I felt myself shrink. I hated this, and I was pretty sure everyone else felt the same. "How are we supposed to catch Scream now?" Master was screaming his head off. "First Krohn, now Marshall! I have been *very* forgiving of your mistakes, but no more. Next thing we know, we'll be losing BogMire!" He sighed and sat down, placing his face in his claws. "What am I supposed to do with you…"

"I can do better. Really," I insisted.

"I sure hope so," he responded coldly, the image of him fading from in front of me.

"RED ALERT! RED ALERT! BogMire is escaping!"

I groaned, my fury building. Not the hatchling again. Seriously? This had gone on long enough. No more fun and games.

NIGHTMARES COME TO LIFE

~SYRYNN~

"Come on, come on, hurry up!"

Ruby, my newest creation, and Spyr were slashing at the metal chains holding BogMire suspended above water like a taunt, the poor two-headed dragon trying to reach his tail for it. I was shooting ice, trying to freeze the chains enough for them to snap while Spyr was shooting...

bubbles? What was that supposed to do?

Suddenly, the bubbles exploded, leaving the chains and cage heavily damaged. He sent another round and they shattered to pieces. BogMire fell into the pool below, slowly lifted one head, and cried out, "We're going to die!" The other head hissed, "Shut up, he'll hear you. Oh, speak of the devil. Now look what you've done."

And that is when I actually saw Shadow. Darkness flowed off him like a cloak, his eyes burning red. His bone-white horns longer than my body, his claws and plated underbelly blood red, the blades on the end of his tails glinting in a wicked spike. He went straight for me, claws outstretched. I was frozen in shock and fear, my brain not hearing all the others screaming my name.

Before his claws could even touch me, Scream was there and Shadow grabbed him instead before he could try anything, teeth sunk right under his jaw. Scream cried out, thrashing, and clawing at Shadow, but the black dragon carried him off as he struggled to get away.

"SCREAM!" Spyr and I wailed, but BogMire stopped us. "We can't do anything for him. Not in our condition." We turned around to head back and help them up, but Ruby blocked our way, her eyes red and her body as big as Shadow's. Please no, not again…

Ruby roared and breathed fire at us. Spyr jumped to the side as I flew above the flames. Spyr ran at her and leapt over the fire as it came at him again, releasing a round of bubbles from his mouth. They exploded on her back, causing her to shriek and swipe at him, knocking him into a wall. I shot shards of ice at her, but she easily melted them. I ran away from her fiery breath, diving behind a metal pillar. She stalked towards me, then hissed as more bubbles exploded in her face. She turned back to Spyr. Whenever she moved to attack Spyr, I would spit electricity at her, and whenever she attacked me, Spyr would blast her with bubbles. We were frustrating her, and she was about to lose it.

She blasted us both against the wall with a torrent of fire and reared back. That is when two blasts of scalding water threw her down the hall, leaving her screaming and thrashing on the floor. BogMire slowly rose up out of the water. His strength was not really back, but it was there, "Come on." He grabbed us in his claws and flew off, leaving an enraged, corrupted Ruby behind. "That should keep her down for a while."

Bog Mire

TRAITORS OF TRAITORS

~SCREAM~

I couldn't move even if I tried. There were a ridiculous amount of chains holding me in place. I couldn't sit, I couldn't move my neck, I couldn't lift anything, and I really had to pee. This was torture. I glared at the shape in the shadows; I had been for at least an hour now.

"Having fun?" He snickered, moving toward me, and revealing my old master. Though last time I had seen him, he wasn't so...

Dead.

"Hello Darkness, my old friend," my voice was dripping with sarcasm.

He smirked, his image flickering a little. "Fine. Use the nickname. Too afraid to say Sephtis?"

"No. You just don't deserve the pleasure of hearing your name spoken by anyone but you. Least of all from me."

"Have it your way." He moved out of the way, so Shadow was now visible.

I narrowed my eyes at him. "Traitor."

Before Shadow could defend himself, Sephtis cut him off. "That may be a bit hypocritical, don't you think?"

I fired back, "Yeah, that is a bit hypocritical coming from you. You know, the one betraying all Dragonkind."

Shadow appeared confused; so, he hadn't told the

poor boy everything. Figured as much. He was good at omitting details like that. Shadow looked to his "master" for an explanation, which came out as smooth as the flammable slime on BogMire's scales. "You know Scream lies."

Like he was doing right now. But that seemed to be enough explanation for Shadow. I growled. "How can you feel right betraying your own kind?"

Shadow actually lowered his head at my demand, but Sephtis didn't seem to notice. He was too busy relishing the fact that I was in chains. "Well, this has been a touching reunion and all, but it's about time the fun started." He looked to a few imps with a sneer. They grinned and pulled a lever.

And then all I felt was crippling pain. Everywhere.

RESCUE NOT-SO-MUCH PARTY

~SPYR~

Syrynn had been angry at Marshall. Very, very angry. In fact, I had never seen someone so angry at Marshall before. They had this big argument since Scream was taken by the evil dragon. Apparently, he had snuck out because he had noticed the scars on Syrynn's face and no longer approved of her going, especially since Marshall had explained what kept happening and that her own creation had poisoned her.

This caused Syrynn to round up a rescue party without telling the adults. They were definitely not going to say yes to all this, since Shadow had taken Scream directly to his fortress in the sky. The adults were still drained and not ready to storm the hold, and they said it was too high for young dragons like us to even attempt. Apparently, we weren't strong enough yet. We were going to attempt it anyway. Obviously. Leave it to Big Sister to be stubborn.

I introduced her to one of the hatchlings that I had made friends with; they had found her egg abandoned on the beach before the attack on the ruins. Tide was a white dragon with blue and green wave designs on her shoulders, horns, and flank. Syrynn let her come because we were going to need all the help we could get, and she liked my super-secret plan. I needed Tide in order to do it, though.

We gathered a whole bunch of dragons: Shade, Callie, Pyre, and Nyxx (Ivy was gonna kill us), Syrynn, me, and Syrynn's newest creation named Emerald. He was HUGE and emerald green with brown horns, black spots on his face, emeralds in his skin, long black claws, and a spike ball tail. His tail was so cool, I wanted a spike ball tail. He was probably the only adult dragon that was going on this secret mission, though he acted like a hatchling. This was gonna be awesome.

Hehe, sorry, I keep getting off-topic. So, we left while the others were sleeping and were deep in the forest. We kept having to shush Shade and Callie the entire time. They were giggling hysterically; you could tell they've never done anything rebellious before.

We stopped at a clearing well away from the ruins and very close to the spot in the sky that Shadow had disappeared into. "You sure this is where we're supposed to be?" Tide asked.

Syrynn nodded, "Yep. I can feel it."

"What's that supposed to mean?" Pyre demanded telepathically.

"Means she can feel her other creations close by," Nyxx rolled her eyes.

Syrynn ignored them both and looked to me. "Do your thing."

I nodded as Tide and I sat on either side of Syrynn and concentrated. We opened our mouths, and each began to blow the biggest bubble we could. Once the bubbles both touched, they combined into a bubble big enough to hold Syrynn inside, floating her up. Tide then made a string of water from the bubble to Emerald's tail so Syrynn wouldn't fly away. We repeated this process until all of us were in bubbles and strung to Emerald's tail. Then the big dragon lifted off and flew high into the sky. He couldn't quite carry all of us otherwise. We looked like a whole bunch of balloons on Emerald's tail, and to my pleasant surprise, the bubbles held up well. I was such a genius.

The fortress came into view and boy, was it terrifying. Black rock walls and spires so tall they disappeared into other clouds. It fit Shadow quite nicely, though it was a little cliché for an evil lair. Emerald silently landed right on the doorstep and our bubbles popped and released us. This place radiated terror and threatened to overwhelm us all with it. But I kept it back with my own powers over fear, the others sighing as it dimmed without supposed explanation. My little secret.

"Let's split up. That way we cover more ground." Syrynn examined us all and then created teams: Pyre and

Nyxx went with Syrynn. Shade and Callie were with Emerald (probably to keep them out of harm's way), and Tide was with me. Shade and Callie were giggling like the children they were when they saw Tide was on my team. Ugh! Immature lizards.

    I rolled my eyes as we headed down the third hallway, still stuck on their dumb behavior. Just because she was my friend didn't mean there was anything else there, but only those two seemed to think differently. I glanced at Tide. Sure, she was slender, and her scales shone like pearls, and her wings were like solidified water and really cool-looking...

    And then her ocean eyes were looking directly in mine and I realized, to my eternal horror, that I was staring. Flustered and embarrassed, I turned my head the other way, feeling the skin under my scales grow hot. She giggled at me. No! This was terrible! Why was she on my team?

We both skidded to a stop once the hall ended at a chamber, and what we saw was the stuff of nightmares. Scream was chained down from head to tail, crying and trembling as the chains hurt him. This black fog was swirling around him and trying to force its way inside him as well, these freaky voices whispering out of it and calling to him. Just like the voices in my head.

Tide was already looking for a way to get him out, finding a lever and pulling it the other way. The power shut off and Scream almost fell over, the chains catching him as his scales emitted steam. How long had they been doing this to him? We used our bubble powers to blast apart the chains, scrambling for cover as he crashed to the floor.

I slowly approached him. "Scream?"

His eyes were entirely red for a moment before the

color receded back into his irises, "...Tide? Spyr?" We grinned at him, the black fog dissipating around him as he smiled back, then frowned. "What are you two... how did you get here?"

I giggled. "Syrynn is so smart. She got us here." He immediately forced himself to his feet at that, causing me and Tide to back up a bit.

Tide attempted to get him to slow down. "You're weak. You're not ready to-" but he took off down the corridor before she could finish. We called after him and gave chase, hoping we didn't run into any trouble.

Which is exactly what we ran into, of course. The others were fighting Shadow and his minions. And they were getting hammered. Shade and Callie got smashed against the wall by Misty's tail, lying on the floor as she trapped them in her talons like a cage. Emerald's scales were smoking, and he was lying on the ground with Ruby standing over him, victorious. Pyre and Nyxx were trapped in a corner by Fizz.

Tide ran in, blasting Ruby with a torrent of water. Ruby shrieked and sputtered as steam rose from her scales. Shadow landed in front of Tide, whipping around so his tails cracked against her and sent her flying into a pillar and smashing it to rubble. She slumped over and Shadow turned away from her. We were so underprepared for this. How did we ever think we were ready to face these monsters?

The largest dragon I had ever seen was facing off Syrynn, his body a swirl of different colored energies, from red and yellow to green and purple. He must have been temporarily using the energy he gathered so he could fight too.

"I have been looking forward to ending you for a

long time," He laughed wickedly. Syrynn couldn't even get up, lying by a large hole in the wall as pieces of it fell and disappeared into the clouds below, her body bruised and battered, bleeding all over the floor.

I don't even remember moving, but suddenly I was the one the large dragon hit with the laser breath that shot from his mouth, my talons spread wide trying to hold it back as my feet slid slightly backwards at the force of it. He kept it coming with a growl as I continued to block it, straining against it so it wouldn't touch my sister.

Pyre and Nyxx slipped underneath and around Fizz and ran to my aid. Scream couldn't do anything but lean against the wall and watch helplessly. Pyre and Nyxx ran underneath the bad dragon, Nyxx blasting shadowy stuff at him and Pyre blasting fire at the earthy energy, weakening it. Without taking his focus off me, the bad dragon splashed

Pyre with the blue energy and sent him tumbling, then he smashed the green energy into Nyxx and threw her into Pyre. Both were dazed.

There was only one way to stop him. "Don't," Nyxx responded in my head.

"You see a better way?" I asked.

"You're crazy!" Pyre's voice shouted.

"You're not the first voice in my head to tell me that." I charged up my own breath.

"NO!" Syrynn, Pyre, and Nyxx all cried out in unison as I fired.

SPYR THROUGH THE SOUL

~SHADOW~

Everything happened so fast, I couldn't tell what was going on. I had to backtrack to remember. The weird little green dragon- Spyr? I don't know- jumped in front of Syrynn. I had stayed back because the situation had appeared to be handled. The toddler dragons, Shade and Callie, had been struggling to get out of my partner Misty's grasp. The twins had run to the green dragon's aid. Tide was slowly getting to her feet at that point, but I held her down with one tail. Then a strange blinding light had erupted from the green one's little body. Next thing I knew, white-out. I awoke to everyone lying on the floor, Scream in the hallway, Master groaning a little ways away on his side and completely out of it.

My eyes fell upon the small green dragon. He was lying with his back to me, not really breathing.

"Spyr, no!" Syrynn forced herself to run to him, despite all her injuries. She slid to his side and nudged him with her snout, her voice a whisper, "Spyr...?" He opened his eyes halfway, devoid of light. Strange... when he had run in earlier, there was this permanent little twinkle in his pupils. Now it was gone.

He smiled up at her. "I'm sorry..."

She shook her head. "You don't need to be sorry.

You did nothing wrong."

"Y-yes, I did..." he insisted, trying to lift his head up. A light caught my eye; his tail was starting to sparkle. Then piece by piece, he started to disappear. Before he entirely vanished, he blew a little bubble out of his mouth. Inside was a little sparking fragment of light, a chain of bubbles making it a necklace. "T-to remember me...?" His eyes were hopeful before he ceased to be all together.

I glanced at Tide; the poor water dragon was leaking a river from her eyes. All right, I'll admit it, I had tears too. In fact, I was angry. This wasn't supposed to happen. Nobody else but Syrynn was supposed to die.

Was I being used? As soon as that thought entered my mind, it felt like some of the fog lifted, and I was startled by a sudden blurry flash of a purple muzzle nudging me to my feet. Where had that come from? Was I...finally starting to remember? That meant...

That meant Sephtis had lied to me. Unbridled rage started to fill my entire body. He put that fog there, not some make believe injury. How dare he use me? In my blind rage, I did something that changed my life forever.

COLD HARD TRUTH

~SCREAM~

I strained to make my way over to Syrynn. None of us were in good shape. She had just slipped Spyr's gift around her neck, her head hanging low to the ground. I sighed. "Syrynn, I'm sorry he's gone. I wish I could have-"

"Why did he do it?" Her voice was so soft, cracking at the end. I was stuck on how to answer her question, then reluctantly came to the conclusion that I should have told her in the very beginning. I couldn't leave her in the dark anymore; there wasn't even a mission to focus on anymore.

"He couldn't stand idly by and watch his sister be murdered, now could he?"

Her head shot up to look at me. "Wh-what?!"

Before I could explain, I saw Shadow move across my peripheral vision, directly toward his master. This couldn't be good. I knew that look in his eyes. "Shadow, no…"

BURY THE CASTLE

~SYRYNN~

"LIAR!" Shadow screeched, grabbing my attention in time for me to see his master rising to his feet. I crept closer, the necklace waving back and forth. "I can't believe I blindly trusted you!" His lips were curled back in a snarl and for once, it wasn't at me. I was shocked. What in the world was he talking about?

The wicked dragon had opened his mouth to respond, only to scream as Shadow blasted him in the maw with red energy. This I could definitely get in on; he murdered Spyr. I ran to assist, even though it was weird to be fighting alongside a dragon that had wanted me dead not five minutes ago.

Shadow blasted him again, causing him to stagger back. I shot a volley of icicles into his back legs that were rolling with red energy and sent him staggering the other way with a shriek, Shadow cut the noise short as his tail whipped him in the face and left a gash across his cheek from the blade at the end. We kept him disoriented like this, taking turns attacking him from all sides and dodging his slowpoke body.

Finally, he had enough of us, "YOU DON'T WANT ME AS YOUR MASTER?" He screeched at the top of his lungs, "SO BE IT!" And suddenly he sucked all this dark power out of Shadow. My eyes were blinking in shock as he started to shrink, becoming the same height as me and slumping over, all his energy drained.

I hurried over to him, squirming underneath until he was completely on top of me and rising up, so I was carrying him on my back. He was out cold, totally unconscious. The evil dragon reared back, his maw starting to glow as he glared fiery daggers at me.

This time I wasn't surprised when Scream was immediately in front of me again, his torn wings spread wide. What did surprise me was when he opened his mouth and an unholy scream erupted from his mouth, ridged and visible sound waves tearing through the air and blasting the baddie back, all the energies that made up his body scattering from the disruption. I was pretty sure my eardrums scattered too. So that was why they called him Scream.

The freed energies went wild, bouncing off pillars and breaking apart walls, the whole place starting to rumble and fall. Scream hurried the others to their feet. "We need to get out of here. Now! Go, go, go!"

Everyone strained to obey, still disoriented from the deafening shriek, and rushing down the crumbling halls.

"This place is coming down!" Scream beat his wings and lifted himself into the air, grabbing a few of the dragons and me while Emerald struggled to grab the rest. Both flew us back to the ruins as Shadow's fortress fell from the sky and erupted into flames once it hit the ground, a cloud of smoke and dust billowing up into a mushroom shape. I wiped tears off my snout with my wing. I had the vague hope that my creations had gotten out safely... even if they did belong to the dark side now. If we could free Shadow, maybe we could free them too.

EPILOGUE
~SYRYNN~

It had been weeks since the flying castle had crashed. Shadow was still out of commission, and the others were deciding our punishment for sneaking out and going after Scream. They had even banned Scream from the discussion since it wasn't his call. I glanced at Tide, who was still a mess. In fact, we were all a mess. My tail wrapped around hers and she calmed, sniffling.

Callie was staring at her talons, tail between her legs. "I've never been a bad draggy before…" My heart hurt at that, my eyes wandering back to the circle of adults. They were talking in hushed tones and to my dismay, I couldn't hear a word they were saying. It was torture. Why couldn't they just get it over with and punish us? Yes, we got Spyr killed. Yes, we snuck out after promising not to. Yes, we endangered every single one of us. But we also freed Shadow, took down the fortress, stalled the evil dragon, and saved Scream. That had to count for something... right?

Finally, what seemed like ages later, Marshall made his way over to us. "We need to talk." We all lowered our gaze to the floor, not brave enough to look him in the eyes.

He sighed, opened his mouth to speak, then his head snapped up as he heard a loud, terrified scream. We all froze in place, looking around. I was the first to notice someone was missing.

"SHADE!" We all took off, heading straight to the place it originated from. I could feel everyone's hearts sinking as we came closer and to our destination. We slid to a halt right at the end of the hall, away from everything else:

Shadow's *empty* room.

ABOUT THE AUTHOR

Kristin Calderon was told by her second-grade teacher that she would be a writer someday. As a very young child she would write screen plays with her friends, but she did not begin writing books until she was 12 years old. Through junior high and high school, she joined several writing clubs and artist groups. For her senior project, she chose to work towards publishing the first book that she had written. This is that book. She has been a fan of reading and writing fantasy books her entire life and hopes that you enjoy the world she created for Syrynn.